WHO LIVES IN THE
ZOO?

Illustrated by Lisa Bonforte

A GOLDEN BOOK · NEW YORK

Western Publishing Company, Inc., Racine, Wisconsin 53404

Who lives in this zoo?
Chimpanzees live here, and a mother
gorilla who carries her baby in her arms.

A family of lions live here, too.
The little cubs have spotted coats. But the
spots will fade as the cubs grow older.

The ostrich is the largest bird in the zoo. Ostriches can't fly. But they can run very, very fast.

There are zebras living here.
Zebras look like horses with
black and white stripes.

Who else lives in the zoo?
Camels live here.
In this zoo there are two kinds of camels.
Some have one hump. Others have two.

Hippopotamuses also live in the zoo.
Hippos spend a lot of time floating in the water.

Who plays in this zoo pond?
Sea lions play here. Sea lions
are very good swimmers.

A big white polar bear
climbs out of the pond and
shakes the water from her
shaggy coat.

Giraffes are the tallest animals in the zoo.

Giraffes eat leaves that are high in the trees. They stretch their legs far apart and reach way down for a drink of water.

Tigers live here, too.
Tigers have stripes that help
to keep them hidden in the tall grass.

Does anybody else live in the zoo?
Elephants live here. Elephants have long trunks.

One elephant sprays himself with water. Another is picking up peanuts.

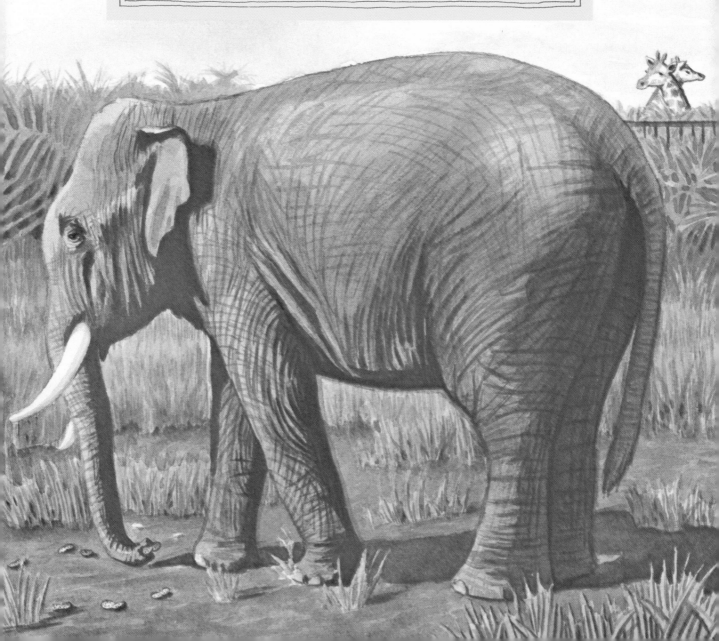

Who lives in the zoo?
All kinds of animals live here.
And many children come to look
at them, every day.